Little Princesses
The Peach Blossom Princess

Little Princesses
The Peach Blossom Princess

By Katie Chase

Illustrated by Leighton Noyes

Red Fox

Special thanks to Narinder Dhami

THE PEACH BLOSSOM PRINCESS
A RED FOX BOOK 9780099488347

First published in Great Britain by Red Fox,
an imprint of Random House Children's Books

This edition published 2006

3 5 7 9 10 8 6 4

Series created by Working Partners Ltd
Copyright © Working Partners Ltd, 2006
Illustrations copyright © Leighton Noyes, 2006
Cover illustration by Nila Aye

All rights reserved. No part of this publication may be reproduced, stored in a
retrieval system, or transmitted in any form or by any means, electronic, mechanical,
photocopying, recording or otherwise, without the prior permission of the publishers.

Set in 15/21pt Bembo Schoolbook

Red Fox Books are published by Random House Children's Books,
61–63 Uxbridge Road, London W5 5SA,
a division of The Random House Group Ltd

Addresses for Random House Group Ltd companies outside the UK
can be found at: www.randomhouse.co.uk

THE RANDOM HOUSE GROUP Limited Reg. No. 954009
www.**kids**at**randomhouse**.co.uk

The Random House Group Limited makes every effort to ensure that the
papers used in its books are made from trees that have been legally
sourced from well-managed and credibly certified forests. Our paper
procurement policy can be found at: www.randomhouse.co.uk/paper.htm.

Mixed Sources
Product group from well-managed
forests and other controlled sources
www.fsc.org Cert no. TT-COC-2139
FSC   © 1996 Forest Stewardship Council

A CIP catalogue record for this book is available from the British Library.

Printed and bound in Great Britain by
Cox & Wyman Ltd, Reading, Berkshire

For David, my best friend

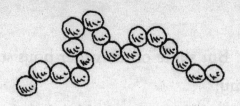

Chapter One

"Hi, Mum." Rosie said, jumping into the front seat of the car, and beaming at her mother and her younger brother. "Hi, Luke."

"You look happy," Mrs Campbell said with a smile as she pulled away from the kerb. "So your first day at your new school went OK then?"

Rosie nodded. "It was great!" she said eagerly. "There are some nice girls in my class – I'm sitting next to one called Megan. And I really like my teacher, Miss Murray." She turned round to glance at her brother. "Did you like your teacher too, Luke?"

Luke pulled a face. "My teacher's OK,"

he said. "But some of the other boys said I talk funny!"

Rosie and her mum couldn't help laughing. "That's because you don't have a Scottish accent," Mrs Campbell remarked, as she drove out of the village. "I'm sure they'll get used to you."

"Oh, I made friends with the boys who were laughing at me," Luke replied cheerfully. "We played football at lunchtime."

"Mum, Miss Murray says our class is putting on a show for the rest of the school," Rosie went on, excitedly. "It's about different countries of the world. We've each been given a country and we have to do a song, poem, dance or reading from that country."

Luke leaned forwards, looking interested. "What's your country?"

"Japan," Rosie replied. "And I don't know *anything* about Japan!"

"Japan," Luke repeated. "Is that near Scotland?"

"No, it's on the other side of the world!" Rosie laughed. "Miss Murray told everyone to look around at home for things that might be useful for the show. I bet Great-aunt Rosamund will have something!"

Rosie's Great-aunt Rosamund had travelled all over the world and she'd filled her Scottish castle with beautiful antiques and treasures from the countries she had visited. She was now away on another long trip, and she had asked Rosie and her family to move into the castle and look after it while she was gone. She had also left a wonderful secret behind for Rosie to discover.

"Oh, yes, your great-aunt is bound to have visited Japan at some point," Mrs Campbell agreed, as she turned into the drive leading to the castle.

Rosie caught her breath as they approached the magnificent grey stone building. Even though they'd been living there for a week or so now, she was still thrilled by the sight of the towers and turrets.

"I think Great-aunt Rosamund *has* been to Japan," Luke said, as the car drew to a halt.

"How do you know?" Rosie asked curiously.

Luke giggled. "I just do!" he replied, and he

jumped out of the car and ran into the castle, through the large wooden door which stood propped open.

"He's up to something!" laughed Mrs Campbell.

"Yes, he's got that look on his face!" Rosie agreed, and she chased after her brother.

Luke was in the Great Hall, a huge room which was packed with Great-aunt Rosamund's treasures. He had a painted fan open in his hand, and when Rosie came in,

he began hopping
about, twisting the
fan around his face.

"Look at me!" he
lisped in a girly
voice. "I'm Rosie,
dancing at the
school show!"

Rosie pulled a face at him, but she had to
laugh. "Where did you find that fan?" she
asked. "It's lovely."

"It was on that table over there," Luke
said, closing it up and handing it to Rosie.
"I was helping Dad tidy in here one day,
and he said it was Japanese."

"Maybe I could do a Japanese dance at
the show, and use the fan," Rosie said
thoughtfully. "I'm sure Great-aunt
Rosamund wouldn't mind if I borrowed it."

"I bet you're not such a good dancer as

me!" Luke laughed cheekily, and
scampered out of the room.

Rosie decided to take the fan
to her bedroom at the top of one
of the castle towers and have a
closer look at it. She hurried
up the winding stairs, and
into the pretty, round
bedroom which had been
her great-aunt's when she
was a little girl. There
Rosie stood in front of
the mirror, and carefully
opened the fan.

The side she was looking
at was a pale sugar-pink,
painted with exotic-looking
birds and butterflies. Rosie
struck a pose, holding the fan
close to her face and peeping over the rim.

Did it make her look at all Japanese?

Suddenly her heart began to race. She had just noticed the reflection of the other side of the fan in the mirror. It was lilac-coloured and had a tree painted on it, its thin, willowy branches dotted with delicate pink blossoms. A girl sat underneath the tree, the flowers falling gently onto her raven-black hair.

"Oh!" Rosie was so surprised, she almost dropped the fan. With trembling fingers she turned it over. "Could this be another little princess?" she asked herself breathlessly.

Great-aunt Rosamund had left a secret note for Rosie, telling her to look out for 'Little Princesses' around the castle. Every time Rosie found one, she ended up having a fantastic adventure. Had she found another princess, here on the Japanese fan?

Rosie stared down at the picture. The girl's head drooped and her eyes were sad, but she

was very richly dressed in a pink kimono,
patterned with white lotus flowers, and a
wide silver sash.

"I'm sure she's a little princess," Rosie said,
holding the fan out in front of her. "But
there's only one way to find out!"

Her eyes fixed on the girl, Rosie followed
Great-aunt Rosamund's instructions and
sank into a curtsey. "Hello!" she said, her
voice trembling with excitement.

Before Rosie had
time to catch her
breath, she felt a warm
breeze shoot out of the
fan and wrap itself
around her. Sugar-pink
blossom petals swirled
in the air, and the bed-
room was filled with
the sweet, warm scent
of ripe peaches. Rosie
closed her eyes and let
the whirlwind pick
her up gently and
whisk her away.
She couldn't wait
to find out where
she was going!

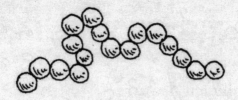

Chapter Two

Rosie kept her eyes closed until she felt her
feet touch down on solid earth again. As the
breeze died away, Rosie finally took a look
around her.

She gasped with delight. She was standing
in one of the most beautiful gardens she had
ever seen. Next to her was a pool, surrounded
by dark rocks, and a river twisting away
from it. Large fish with golden scales swam
slowly here and there in the clear water, and
a little bamboo bridge led from one side
of the pool to the other. Trees laden with
blossoms lined the banks of the pool and
the river, and feathery green ferns with white

and purple flowers grew beneath them. In the distance, Rosie could see the sun glinting off golden rooftops.

"Oh, this is lovely!" Rosie said to herself. For the first time she glanced down and realized, with a thrill of excitement, that her clothes had changed. She was now wearing a snow-white kimono, embroidered with yellow roses. It had long, wide sleeves and reached right down to the floor.

Rosie hurried over to the pool to look at her reflection, taking care not to trip over the hem of her kimono. As she peered into the water, she saw that her hair was piled high on top of her head and secured in place by two golden hair pins with sparkling jewels hanging from the tips

"Now I really do look Japanese!" Rosie said to herself, admiring the way the jewelled pins glittered in the sunshine.

Suddenly, Rosie's heart jumped. She could see the reflection of one of the blossom trees in the water – and she could also see somebody peeping out at her around the trunk of the tree!

Rosie spun round. A girl stood there, in the shadow of the tree. Rosie recognized her straightaway as the girl she had seen on the fan. She wore the same pink kimono and wide silver sash, and she had the same black hair, piled up on her head like Rosie's. She still looked miserable, and Rosie could see that she was crying.

"Hello, what's the matter?" Rosie said kindly. "Can I help?"

A look of shock crossed the girl's tear-stained face. "Oh!" she gasped. "Can you *really* see me?"

Rosie looked puzzled. "Well, of course I can see you!" she said.

The girl's face lit up. Wiping away her tears, she hurried across the path to Rosie and took her hand.

"I don't know how you can see me, but I'm so glad you can!" she said gratefully. "My name is Hana – and I'm the *real* princess!"

"I'm Rosie," said Rosie. "I'm here because my Great-aunt Rosamund told me to look for little princesses – and I found you!"

"My own great-aunt used to have a magic friend called Rosamund who came to visit her when she was a little girl!" Hana exclaimed happily.

"That was my great-aunt!" Rosie laughed.

"And now *you've* come to visit *me!*" Hana beamed at her. "So that means you're *my* magic friend!"

"But why did you think I wouldn't be able to see you?" asked Rosie.

All the happiness fled from Hana's face. "I'm invisible to *everyone!*" she explained in a trembling voice. "Except for you. I suppose you can see me because you're here by magic yourself."

"But why are you invisible?" Rosie asked curiously. "What happened?"

Hana led Rosie over to a grassy bank beside the rock pool, where they sat down under a blossom tree.

"My father is Emperor of Japan," Hana began, "And he's a very powerful man. But he has offended someone even more powerful." She pointed at the dark waters of the river, as it flowed into the rock pool.

"Gawa, the river god."

"How?" Rosie asked.

"My father's
fishermen took pearls
from the riverbed to make a
necklace for my birthday today,"
Hana explained. "But my father didn't make
an offering to Gawa to thank him for the
pearls. The river god was angry, and decided
to take his revenge."

Rosie was fascinated by the little princess's
story. "What did he do?"

Hana smiled sadly. "A few days ago I was
sitting here in my favourite spot under this
peach tree. Suddenly I saw a peach
floating down the river towards
me." She stared out over
the swirling waters. "I love
peaches, Rosie, and this
one was a beauty. I could

see its lovely pink and orange skin, and smell its warm, rich scent. So I took a branch and pulled it out of the river." She sighed. "I didn't know it was a *magic* peach, and that Gawa had sent it."

"A magic peach?" Rosie gasped.

Hana nodded. "I took one of my hairpins and used it to cut the peach open. But as I did so . . ." she faltered. "Rosie, you'll never believe what happened. A girl grew out of the middle of the peach — right there before my eyes! And, Rosie, looking at her was just like looking into a mirror. She was the mirror image of *me*!"

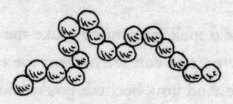

Chapter Three

Rosie's mouth fell open. She was so shocked, she hardly knew what to say. "*Exactly* the same?" she asked Hana.

"From my head to my toes," Hana sighed. "She said she was a water sprite, sent by Gawa to get his pearls back, and that she was going to pretend to be me until my birthday feast, when my father will present her with the necklace."

"So that's why you told me you were the *real* princess!" Rosie said, remembering Hana's words when they'd first met. "Because the sprite is pretending to be *you*!"

"Yes," agreed Hana, wiping away a tear.

"She cast a spell over me to make me invisible. Now no one can see or hear me except the sprite. And you, because you're magical too."

"That's horrible!" Rosie said indignantly. "But you said that today is your birthday, didn't you?"

Hana nodded.

"So the sprite will get the pearls and then she'll take them back to Gawa, and you won't be invisible anymore," Rosie pointed out.

"Yes, I hope so," Hana sighed.

"Hana! Where are you?"

Rosie blinked as a voice came drifting through the trees towards them. It sounded exactly like Hana's.

"That's the sprite!" Hana whispered, looking panic-stricken. "Quickly, Rosie, hide behind the peach tree!"

Jumping up, Rosie darted behind the tree and pressed herself against the trunk, her heart pounding. *Poor Hana*, Rosie thought.

She heard the sound of footsteps coming closer. Curious to see the sprite, she peeped out from behind the tree.

The sprite was walking through the flowers towards Hana. Rosie stared and almost gasped out loud, for the sprite looked like she

could be Hana's twin! She had the same
face, and the same slender figure and jet-
black hair. The only difference was that the
sprite wore a blue kimono embroidered with
silver stars.

The sprite stopped a little way from the
rock pool. "Come here!" she called
imperiously to Hana.

Miserably Hana headed towards the sprite.
Rosie couldn't help wondering why the sprite
didn't walk closer to Hana. It seemed almost
as if she wanted to avoid the water, but that
didn't really make sense – after all, she was a
water sprite. *Maybe she just likes bossing Hana
around*, Rosie thought, beginning to feel very
angry on her friend's behalf.

"Well, now," the sprite said with a smile,
playing with one of her diamond hairpins,
"I didn't know I was going to have such a
lovely time being a princess. It's wonderful

having servants and beautiful clothes and jewellery." She laughed a tinkling laugh. "So I've decided not to go back to the river."

"What?" Hana gasped. Behind the tree, Rosie clapped her hand to her mouth in shock.

"I'm not going back to the river," the sprite repeated. "I'm going to stay here and be Princess Hana for ever!"

"No!" Hana exclaimed, and Rosie could hear the desperation in her friend's voice. "You can't! What about Gawa? He'll still want his pearls back!"

The sprite giggled. "Don't forget that the emperor is giving *me* those pearls for *my* birthday," she said airily. "I couldn't possibly give them to someone else. It would break my father's heart!"

"He's not your father!" Hana cried, tears beginning to roll down her pale cheeks. "He's mine! And I won't be invisible for ever, so your plan won't work!"

A sly look crossed the sprite's face. Bending down, she scooped up a handful of peach blossom from the grass. Then she flung the petals over Hana, murmuring a few words under her breath.

"There!" The sprite said, smiling spitefully at the princess. "My spell is done. Now you *will* be invisible for ever!"

"No!" Hana sobbed.

The sprite stared at her thoughtfully.

"Well, maybe not completely invisible . . ." she said, with a laugh. "People will smell the scent of peach blossom whenever you are near!"

And, laughing merrily, the sprite turned and skipped away.

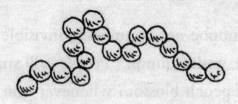

Chapter Four

Rosie hurried over to her friend.

"Did you see what happened, Rosie?" Hana asked. "What am I going to do?"

"Don't worry," Rosie said comfortingly, slipping her arm around the unhappy princess. "We'll think of a way to outwit that horrible sprite."

"But how?" Hana asked miserably.

Rosie thought for a moment. "Well, we can't do it without magic, so we must speak to Gawa the river god," she said at last. "We'll need his help."

Hana nodded and led Rosie over to the riverbank, where they both knelt down on the springy green grass.

"Lean forward and touch the water with your fingertips," Hana told Rosie softly.

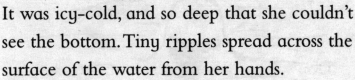

Rosie touched the surface of the river with her fingers. It was icy-cold, and so deep that she couldn't see the bottom. Tiny ripples spread across the surface of the water from her hands.

"Gawa the powerful," Hana began to chant, "Gawa the strong, Gawa the masterful, please hear my song . . ."

Rosie joined in, and together the girls recited the chant again and again. After a while, Rosie saw that the ripples on the surface of the water were getting bigger and stronger. Suddenly the dark water began to bubble furiously right in the middle of the river. The next moment, the waters grew calm and still and a face appeared.

"Who dares to waken the great river god from his sleep?" demanded a booming voice.

Rosie couldn't help feeling a little scared as she stared at Gawa's angry face. He had long black hair tied up in a topknot, and a long black beard which rippled in the flowing waters of the river. His piercing dark eyes were fixed on Rosie and Hana.

"Answer me!" he roared.

"It's me, great Gawa." Hana said quickly, bowing low. "Hana, the emperor's daughter."

"And who is this?" Gawa growled, glaring at Rosie. "I am a very important god. I don't have time for little girls!"

Rosie bowed too. "I'm Hana's friend," she explained. "We called you because the sprite you sent to get your pearls isn't coming back to the river. She's planning to take Hana's place permanently and keep the pearls for herself."

Gawa's face darkened. "I knew I shouldn't have trusted that sprite!" he muttered.

"Gawa, we need your help to defeat her," Rosie begged, "or Hana will be invisible for ever."

"Why should *I* help?" the river god muttered sulkily. "No one cared when my pearls were stolen from me without even a thank you from the emperor!" He looked at Rosie, a sneer on his face. "Stop wasting my time!"

To Rosie's alarm, the water began to bubble again, and Gawa's reflection started to fade. Rosie bit her lip, anxiously. What *could* she say to make Gawa agree to help?

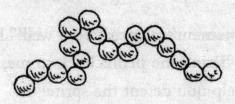

Chapter Five

Hana looked at Rosie in dismay.

Rosie could only think of one thing to do. "Great Gawa!" she cried, as the river god's face was about to vanish. "Please wait!"

Gawa's grumpy face slowly began to reappear. "Why?" he demanded.

"If you help us defeat the sprite," Rosie gabbled quickly, afraid that the god would disappear before she finished, "I promise we'll get your pearls back!"

She heard Hana gasp beside her, but Rosie stared hard at Gawa, willing him to agree.

"So you'll return my pearls," the river god said thoughtfully, stroking his beard. There was a moment's silence. "Very well!" he roared. "Bring the pearls back to me, and I will help you defeat the sprite!"

Rosie sighed with relief.

"But if you fail, don't expect any help from me!" Gawa snapped. And, with that, the river began to bubble again and his face faded away.

"Rosie, you were very brave!" Hana said gratefully. "But we don't have much time. My birthday feast starts a few hours from now, and we must get the necklace before my father presents it to the sprite."

"Do you know where the necklace is kept?" asked Rosie.

Hana nodded. "In my father's study," she replied. "But you'll have to pick it up and take it to Gawa, Rosie. I can't hold anything now that I'm invisible."

"Don't worry," Rosie said reassuringly.

"Just show me where the pearls are."

"Follow me!" Hana cried. She hurried off along one of the paths, with Rosie close behind her. As they wove their way through the gardens, Rosie saw that they were heading towards the golden rooftops which she'd noticed earlier.

They reached a red archway guarded by two huge statues of golden dragons.

Rosie stopped to stare in awe. "This is like something in a storybook!" she sighed, peering through the arch.

A pagoda palace stood on the other side of a large courtyard, and it was magnificent. Slender pillars supported the sweeping, curled rooftops of gold, and each roof was elaborately decorated with carvings of dragons. The walls of the building were

adorned with carved friezes, and the great red doors were painted with pictures of birds, animals and flowers.

"Wait here," Hana whispered, drawing Rosie into the shadow of one of the dragon statues. Then she darted into the courtyard, checked that the coast was clear, and beckoned to Rosie.

"This way," Hana whispered, leading Rosie to a small side door.

Rosie opened the door and the girls slipped inside. They were in a marble corridor, and a delicious, savoury smell filled the air. Rosie could also hear the *clink* of dishes, and guessed that they were close to the kitchens.

Hana led Rosie along the winding corridor. "This will take us to my father's study," she explained, pointing at a flight of golden stairs in front of them.

"We're lucky there aren't many people around," Rosie whispered as they began to climb the stairs.

"All the servants are in the kitchens, preparing for my birthday feast," Hana explained.

But as they reached the top of the stairs, Rosie suddenly heard footsteps approaching. Hana turned pale. "In here!" she whispered, pointing at the nearest door.

Rosie pushed the door open, and hurried into the room. She just had time to notice that she was in a beautiful bedroom before Hana ushered her out of sight behind an ebony screen, inlaid with mother-of-pearl butterflies.

"This is my bedroom," Hana whispered to Rosie, as the footsteps came closer. "But now the sprite thinks it's hers!"

Rosie's heart pounded as she realized that the approaching stranger was coming in! She peered through the tiny, decorative holes in the side of the screen, trying to see who it was.

It was the river sprite. She swept into the room, followed by four servants who all looked rather miserable.

"I must choose a kimono for my birthday feast," said the sprite haughtily. "Lay out my best clothes in the next room, so I can view them."

"Yes, Highness," the servants mumbled.

"Be off with you then!" the sprite snapped. The servants turned and rushed from the room, almost colliding with more servants who were bringing in large copper jugs of hot water.

"It's time for your bath, Highness," one of them said nervously.

The sprite waved her hand at the porcelain bath in the corner. "Fill it up then!" she said irritably.

The servants hurried over to the bath and began filling it with water. Unfortunately, one of them was so nervous that he spilt a little water on the floor near her feet.

"How dare you?" the sprite screamed furiously, jumping backwards. "I'm far too upset to have a bath now. Get out, all of you!"

The servants almost fell over each other in their eagerness to escape. Behind the screen, Hana pulled a face at Rosie.

"The sprite's horrible to my poor servants," she whispered angrily. "They must wonder why I've changed so much!"

Rosie peeped out again. The sprite was now seated at Hana's dressing table. The table was covered with heaps of shiny bottles, glittering jewels and sparkly hairpins, all tangled up together.

Rosie watched as the sprite unpinned her long black hair and began brushing it with a diamond-studded comb. The glitter of the diamonds in the sunlight seemed to mesmerize her.

"Look at the mess she's made of my dressing table!" Hana grumbled crossly. "She's spoiling all my things!"

Suddenly there was a timid knock on the door.

"Come in!" the sprite shouted.

One of the servants hurried into the room and bowed. "Highness, your kimonos are ready for you to inspect," she said.

"And about time too!" the sprite declared. She put the comb down, giving the diamonds one last, loving look, and swept out of the door with the servant girl.

"We'd better get out of here while she's gone," Rosie said urgently. "We must get the pearls and we don't have much time."

Hana nodded, following Rosie out of the bedroom. They tiptoed along the corridor, passed the room next door – where they could hear the sprite complaining loudly to the servants that they'd creased her favourite kimono – and round the corner.

"This is my father's study," Hana said, stopping outside another set of doors. "But he won't be in there now, he'll be in his dressing room getting ready for the feast."

Rosie opened the door and the girls went inside. The study was lined with shelves holding hundreds of rolls of parchment, and there was an enormous wooden desk and a golden chair carved in the shape of a dragon.

"Over here," Hana said in a low voice.

She pointed at a heavy tapestry which hung on the wall. "Put your hand behind the tapestry, Rosie."

Rosie did so, and was surprised to discover a hole neatly cut into the wall. Her fingers closed around a box, and she pulled it out.

"The pearls are inside," Hana told her.

The box was made of different coloured woods, put together neatly to form intricate patterns. There was a panel on top to open the box. Rosie tried to slide it off, but it wouldn't move.

"It's stuck!" Rosie panted, trying to pull the panel this way and that without success.

Hana laughed. "It's a Japanese puzzle box," she explained. "It's for keeping valuable things safe. No one can open it unless they line up all the tiles properly to make a picture. Start here, Rosie." Hana pointed at one side of the box. "Now, slide the bottom panel across."

Rosie hadn't realized that the box was made up of small sliding panels. She moved the one Hana had indicated.

"And now this one," Hana said, pointing at another panel.

Twenty moves later, Rosie gave a gasp of triumph as the tiles fell into place to form a picture of a lion. Now the top panel slid open easily, and there, nestling on a bed of blue velvet, lay a string of lustrous, creamy pearls.

"Great!" Rosie declared. She tucked the pearls into the pocket of her kimono, then replaced the open box behind the tapestry.

"Now we return to Gawa," Hana said happily.

But as the girls hurried out into the corridor, they froze in horror. They could hear the sound of voices!

"Rosie, it's my father!" Hana exclaimed, looking panic-stricken. "And he's coming this way! You must hide!"

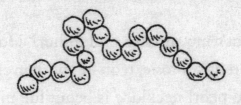

Chapter Six

Rosie turned to run back into the study, but Hana shook her head.

"Not in there, Rosie! My father must be coming to fetch the pearls!" She pointed at a suit of armour which stood opposite the doorway. "Hide behind that!"

Rosie dived out of sight just in time. A man dressed in red robes trimmed with gold appeared around the corner of the corridor. He was accompanied by a woman in a flowing pink silk kimono, patterned with darker pink blossoms, and they were followed by two stern-looking guards wearing black armour.

"That's my mother and father," Hana whispered to Rosie, tears filling her eyes.

"The pearl necklace is beautiful, my dear," the emperor was saying as they approached the study. "I hope Hana will like it."

"Yes." The empress frowned slightly. "Do you think our Hana is quite well at the moment? She hasn't seemed herself for the last few days."

"She has been quite bad-tempered," the emperor admitted, "Which isn't like dear Hana at all!"

Tears rolled down Hana's cheeks and Rosie patted her arm.

Just as the emperor and his wife reached the study, the empress stopped and sniffed the air.

"I can smell peaches!" she said with a smile. "The servants must have gathered some blossoms to scent the ballroom. They

know how much Hana loves peach blossom!"

Rosie smiled sympathetically at her friend who was wiping away her tears.

"You must get away while they are inside the study," Hana whispered to her. "Before my father finds out that the pearls are missing."

Rosie nodded. As the guards followed the emperor and his wife into the study, Rosie slipped out from behind the suit of armour.

But, as she crept away, she heard an angry shout.

"The pearls! They're gone!" cried the emperor.

"Let's get out of here!" Rosie panted, as she raced down the corridor with Hana close behind.

Hana led Rosie back to the door where they had entered the palace, but as they peeped round the corner of the corridor to check that there was no one around, they

 saw that a guard had been placed there. Rosie just managed to duck out of sight before he turned his head and spotted her.

"What now?" she whispered to Hana. But her voice came out a little louder than she'd intended.

"Who's there?" the guard at the door called sharply.

Hana popped her head round the corner.

"The guard's coming this way!" she gasped. "Quick, Rosie, hide!"

Panicking, Rosie glanced around her. To her left, two huge golden doors stood wide open. She scurried towards them.

"Be careful!" Hana warned anxiously. "That's the ballroom where the feast is taking place. It might be full of servants!"

But there was nowhere else to go. Rosie dived through the doors, praying that there wouldn't be any servants to catch her. To her relief she saw that the room was empty, except for the banqueting tables piled high with food, and one young boy who was working at the largest table. He was putting the final touches to a huge ice sculpture of a swan, which was the centrepiece of the

display, and he didn't even notice Rosie.

Trying not to make a sound, Rosie lifted up one of the white tablecloths and scrambled beneath the table. She let the cloth fall again, hiding her from view.

A moment later she saw the guard's feet appear in the doorway. He walked around

and then moved away. Rosie breathed a sigh of relief and then realized that Hana wasn't with her. She lifted the tablecloth slightly and peeped out into the room. Where was the little princess?

To her surprise, she saw that her friend was standing next to the young ice sculptor,

watching him sadly. The boy was still
chipping away at the swan's graceful neck,
but as Rosie watched, he turned his head
and sniffed the air. Rosie guessed that even
though he couldn't see Hana, he could smell
the scent of peach blossom.

"Jiro!" Just then the guard rushed into
the ballroom again. "Jiro, you must come

quickly! The princess's pearl necklace has been stolen, and the emperor says that everyone must help search for the thief!"

"Oh!" Jiro jumped up, putting his chisel away in his belt. "I'll come right away."

Rosie stayed beneath the table until Jiro and the guard had hurried out of the room. Then she peeked out again.

Still looking upset, Hana hurried over to her. "That's Jiro, the ice sculptor's son," she explained. "He's my best friend, and even he can't see me!"

"Not for much longer, though," Rosie pointed out in a determined voice. "As soon as we get back to Gawa, he'll help us break the spell. Come on, we must go."

"Let me see if the corridor is clear," said Hana, running to the doorway. She popped her head outside, and then ran back to Rosie, her face pale. "Rosie, the palace is swarming with guards looking for the pearls! You'll have to stay hidden!"

Rosie shrank back under the tablecloth. It seemed she was well and truly trapped!

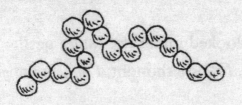

Chapter Seven

A few moments later, a crowd of servants and guests bustled into the ballroom looking for the stolen necklace. Rosie stayed where she was, hoping that no one would think to look under the tables. Hana joined her and the two of them sat there and waited.

The whole palace was in uproar. From her hiding place, Rosie could hear footsteps running here and there, and the sound of doors opening and closing.

Two servants stopped near Rosie's table.

"Well the thief isn't in here!" said one. "Let's go and look somewhere else."

"Wait a minute," the other replied. "We

haven't looked under the tables yet."

Oh, no! Rosie thought, *I'm going to get caught!*

But just at that moment, one of the servants sounded a loud, brass gong, and, peeking out from under the cloth, Rosie saw everyone bow as the emperor swept into the room. He was followed by a crowd of guards, servants and courtiers.

Everybody fell quiet as the emperor began to speak. "The pearl necklace has not been recovered!" he announced. "I am therefore postponing my daughter's birthday feast until tomorrow evening." Everyone

began murmuring to each other, and the emperor raised his hand for silence. "Without the necklace, my daughter will not have a special present," he went on, "so if anyone can bring my precious Hana a gift even more beautiful and spectacular than the pearl necklace, I will grant that person their heart's desire!"

Everyone burst into excited conversation as the emperor left the room. As they began to file out after him, Rosie turned to Hana.

"This is my chance," she whispered. "If I leave now, everyone will think I'm just one of the guests."

Hana nodded. "Be careful!" she whispered.

As the last group made their way to the door, Rosie and Hana slipped out from under the table and joined the crowd. The guests were busily discussing the emperor's speech; they didn't notice that an extra person had appeared. Rosie and Hana walked with the guests out into the courtyard. Then Rosie strolled casually through the arch and into the gardens.

She heaved a huge sigh of relief. "Come on, Hana!" she said. "Let's take the pearls back to Gawa."

The sun was sinking in the sky, turning the horizon pink and gold, as the two girls ran back to the riverbank. There, Rosie dipped her fingers in the water and repeated the chant which had summoned the river god earlier.

Rosie held her breath as the water began

to bubble and once again the grumpy face of Gawa appeared.

"What do you want this time?" growled the river god.

Rosie held up the string of creamy pearls. "We have the necklace!" she said triumphantly.

Gawa's face lit up. "Throw them into the river," he ordered, "so that what is rightfully mine is restored to me!"

Rosie tossed the pearls into the river. As soon as they touched the water, it began to bubble, sucking the pearls beneath the surface.

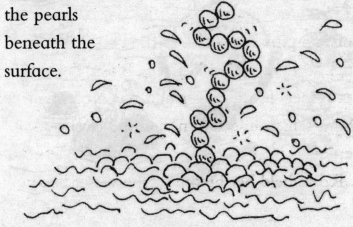

Gawa smiled with satisfaction. But then, to Rosie's horror, his face began to fade.

"Wait!" Rosie cried. "You promised to help us defeat the sprite!"

"Oh, yes." Gawa yawned, looking very uninterested. His face was still fading, even as he spoke. "Get her wet and she will return to her natural form. She will become a water sprite again, and her spell will be broken."

Rosie frowned. "But how can we do that?" she asked anxiously. "We'll never get near the sprite because of the guards, and anyway, she hates water. She won't go near it!"

"That's not my problem," Gawa snapped. "I've fulfilled my part of the bargain!" And he began to fade away to nothing.

Rosie racked her brains. There *had* to be a way to get the sprite wet. "Please don't go!" she begged, as a plan began to form in her head. "I've had an idea — but we'll need your help once more, oh Gawa!"

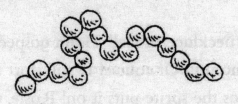

Chapter Eight

Gawa hesitated. For a moment it looked as if he might fade away entirely, and Rosie and Hana both held their breath. But at last, curiosity got the better of him and he began to reappear.

"Tell me your plan," he ordered, "And then I will decide if I will honour you with my help!"

"Thank you," Rosie said bowing. Hana was looking at her curiously too, so Rosie began to explain. "I've noticed that the sprite loves shiny, sparkly things," Rosie said. "So we'll ask Jiro, the ice sculptor's son, to carve us a beautiful necklace of ice."

"A necklace of ice!" Hana gasped, her face lighting up. "Of course! It will start to melt as soon as the sprite puts it on! Rosie, that's brilliant!"

"But we will need a magic box to keep the necklace frozen until we present it to the sprite," Rosie went on. "That's why we need your help, great Gawa."

Gawa frowned. "Your idea might work," he said thoughtfully. "But what's in it for me?"

Rosie didn't know what to say, but Hana quickly stepped forwards.

"My father has promised that he will grant the person who brings the most beautiful gift their heart's desire," she told the river god. "If the sprite chooses our necklace, we will ask my father to build an enormous temple in your honour."

"Oh, I like the sound of that!" Gawa murmured with a smug smile. "Very well.

I'll help you!" Rosie and Hana beamed at each other. "Princess, do you have the stone from the magic peach?"

Hana nodded and drew the peach stone from the pocket of her kimono.

"Place it on the surface of the water," Gawa ordered.

Hana did so. The peach stone bobbed on the surface of the river. Then it began to spin, growing in size and sparkling with magic. A few moments later, the stone had turned into a beautiful silver box with a swirly, watery pattern running around the sides of it.

"Take the box," Gawa said, briskly. Then he frowned. "I look forward to seeing that ungrateful sprite when she returns to my river!"

"Thank you, Gawa," Rosie and Hana called, as the river god faded from sight altogether.

Rosie reached into the river to pick up the box. "Oh!" she gasped, as her fingers closed around it. "It's cold!" She opened the box and touched the dark blue silk lining. That felt even colder.

"Now we must ask Jiro to carve the ice necklace," Hana said. She glanced up at the pale moon in the dark night sky. "But that will have to wait till morning. Let's try to get some sleep, Rosie."

The two girls lay down beneath the peach tree on a soft carpet of blossom. It seemed to Rosie like only a few minutes later that Hana was gently shaking her shoulder and whispering "Wake up, Rosie!"

"Oh!" Rosie sat up and yawned. It was dawn, and she could already feel the warmth of the early morning sun. "Shall we go and find Jiro?"

Hana nodded. "He'll be in the ice house," she replied. "The ice sculptors need to stack the ice before it gets too warm."

Rosie climbed to her feet and straightened her kimono. Then Hana led her down a winding path through the gardens.

"The ice house is outside the palace courtyard," Hana explained. "So we don't have to worry about being spotted."

"Hana, do you think Jiro will believe me when I explain why we need the necklace?" Rosie asked, suddenly feeling nervous. "After all, he won't be able to see you."

"We'll just have to convince him!" Hana replied in a determined voice. "Here we are."

The ice house was situated in a shady part of the gardens, surrounded by tall trees. It was built of stone, and had a sweeping rooftop, like the palace.

"Open the door, Rosie," Hana said.

Rosie did so, and immediately felt herself surrounded by an icy chill. Jiro was inside, stacking large blocks of ice, one on top of the other.

"Who's there?" he asked, turning round quickly.

"My name's Rosie," Rosie replied, trying not to shiver. "I'm a friend of Princess Hana's and I need to talk to you."

Jiro stared at her in surprise. "Well, come inside and shut the door then," he said, "or the ice will melt."

Rosie and Hana stepped inside and Rosie closed the door. The temperature in the ice house was freezing. Icicles hung from the roof, and even the floor felt cold and slippery beneath Rosie's feet. She wrapped her arms around herself, trying to keep warm. Jiro, who was dressed in a thin shirt, didn't seem to notice the chill.

"You say you're a friend of Princess Hana?" Jiro said, looking a little suspicious. "But I've never seen you before. What do you want?"

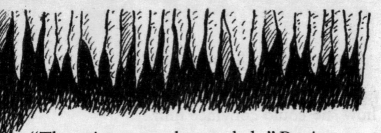

"The princess needs your help," Rosie explained. "She's in trouble."

Jiro looked confused. "But I've just seen the princess in the palace," he declared. "She ignored me. She's been doing that a lot over the last few days!" He sounded very hurt.

Hana sighed and shook her head at Rosie. "That's because she's not the real princess!" Rosie replied firmly. Then, before Jiro could speak, she quickly went on to tell him the whole story. "And the only way to get rid of the sprite is to get her wet, that's why we need the ice necklace," Rosie finished. "Then Hana won't be invisible any more."

Jiro frowned. "Is this a joke?"

"No!" Rosie said desperately, wondering how she could convince him.

"Rosie," Hana said suddenly, "ask Jiro if he remembers carving an ice butterfly for my birthday last year. It was a special present. No one knew of it except the two of us."

"OK," Rosie agreed, turning back to Jiro who was staring at her in amazement.

"Who are you talking to?" he asked.

"The princess," Rosie replied. "She's right here next to me."

Jiro shook his head. "I think you'd better go—" he began.

"Hana says that you carved an ice butterfly for her birthday last year!" Rosie broke in.

"How could you know that?" Jiro gasped. "No one knew except the princess and me!" He stared at the empty space next to Rosie. "Is the princess *really* invisible?"

"Yes," Rosie said. "But can you smell the scent of peach blossom?"

Jiro sniffed the air. "Yes, I can," he said wonderingly.

"That means Hana is close by!" Rosie told him. "Now, can you help us break the spell, Jiro? Will you carve the necklace?"

Jiro hesitated, then nodded. "I thought something wasn't right with the princess," he said slowly. "If she was really a sprite, that explains it. Yes, I'll carve the necklace!"

Rosie and Hana glanced at each other in delight.

"Oh, thank you!" Rosie said. She took Gawa's magic box out of her pocket and gave it to Jiro. "If you put the necklace in here, it will stay frozen until we give it to the sprite."

Jiro nodded, looking worried. "The necklace will have to be really beautiful to fool her. I've never carved anything so complicated before," he said.

"Just do your best." Rosie replied, and as she and Hana left the ice house, she hoped that it would be enough.

Chapter Nine

"Jiro is a wonderful ice sculptor," Hana told
Rosie as they sat beneath the peach tree.
"I'm sure he'll carve a beautiful necklace."

"I hope so," Rosie replied.

The two girls had spent the day in the
gardens. Now the sun was setting, the moon
was rising, and it was almost time for the
birthday celebrations to begin.

"Let's go to the ice house," Hana said.
"Jiro will have the necklace ready for us
by now."

As the two girls hurried through the
gardens, Rosie wondered if the ice necklace
would be realistic enough to fool the sprite.

And even if it is, she thought, *what if she chooses someone else's gift?*

Jiro was waiting for the girls outside the ice house. He beamed at Rosie. "What do you think?" he asked, holding up a string of sparkling, icy diamonds.

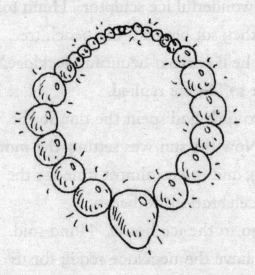

Rosie caught her breath. The necklace was beautiful. Each piece of ice had been carefully cut and polished to reflect the light this way and that. Then the ice diamonds had been strung together, with the largest ones in the middle and smaller ones radiating outwards. Jiro had even carved a clasp of solid ice to fasten the necklace.

"They look just like real diamonds!" Hana gasped.

"They're beautiful!" Rosie cried, clapping her hands.

Jiro looked pleased. "Wait till you see it in the light of the torches at the feast," he said, laying the necklace carefully in its icy, silver box. "Then it will sparkle even brighter than real diamonds!" He glanced at the space next to Rosie. "Does the princess like it?" he asked shyly.

"She loves it!" Rosie assured him, as Hana nodded enthusiastically. "Thank you, Jiro."

"May the luck of the gods be with you," Jiro called after the girls as they hurried away.

When Rosie and Hana reached the palace courtyard, Rosie could hardly believe her eyes. "Look!" she gasped, pointing at the palace.

A long procession of people snaked around the courtyard. They were carrying baskets and boxes and parcels in richly-coloured wrapping

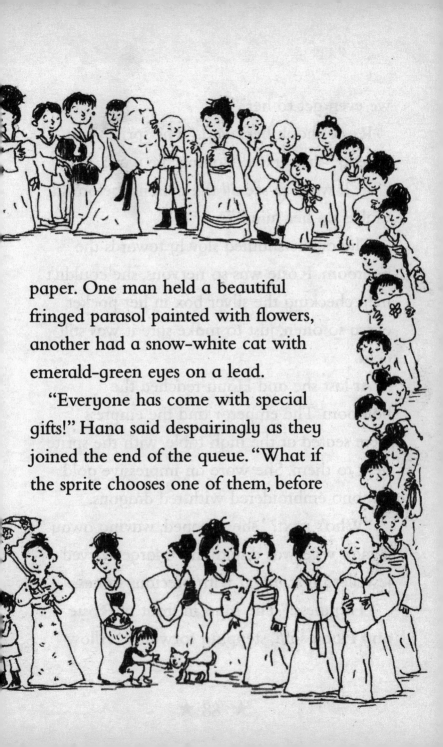

paper. One man held a beautiful
fringed parasol painted with flowers,
another had a snow-white cat with
emerald-green eyes on a lead.

"Everyone has come with special
gifts!" Hana said despairingly as they
joined the end of the queue. "What if
the sprite chooses one of them, before

we even get to her?"

Rosie shook her head. "The sprite's too greedy," she replied, hoping she was right. "She'll want to see *all* the presents before she makes up her mind!"

The queue shuffled slowly towards the ballroom. Rosie was so nervous, she couldn't help checking the silver box in her pocket every so often, just to make sure it was still cold.

At last she and Hana reached the ballroom. The emperor and the empress were seated at the high table, with the sprite next to them. She wore an impressive gold kimono embroidered with red dragons.

"Who's next?" she snapped, waving away a man who was displaying a large, carved jewellery box inlaid with precious stones.

"Highness!" The man in front of Rosie and Hana said, stepping forwards. "Allow

me to present you with a set of glittering
rubies!"

The sprite looked interested as the man
opened a green silk bag and drew out the
rubies. Rosie and Hana glanced at each
other in dismay, for the stones were stunning,
each one glowing with a deep red fire.

"Lovely!" The sprite said, clapping her
hands gleefully. "I might choose your gift.

But, then again, I might not!" She looked beyond the man at Rosie. "What is your birthday present to me, girl?" she demanded imperiously.

Rosie bowed, reaching into her pocket for the silver box. "Highness, I have come from far, far away and I have brought you the most dazzling gems the world has ever seen!"

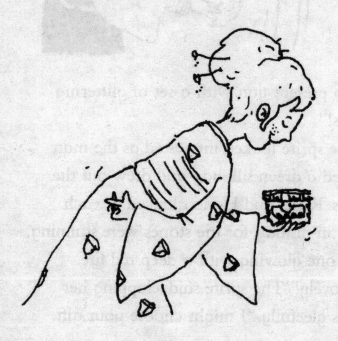

The sprite leaned forwards, her eyes shining greedily. "Let me see!"

Trying to stay calm, Rosie opened the box and held it out so the sprite could see the necklace. Behind her back she quietly crossed her fingers. Would the icy diamonds win the river sprite's icy heart?

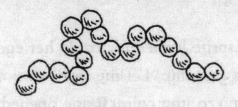

Chapter Ten

"*Oh!*"

As Rosie let the lid of the box fall back, it wasn't just the sprite who gasped in awe. Everyone in the ballroom sighed in wonder at the fiery glow of the ice diamonds. They lay glittering on the dark blue silk, like stars in the night sky. The golden torchlight reflected off each tiny facet, sending rainbows of sparkling light into every corner of the ballroom. Even Rosie caught her breath as she saw the diamonds again.

"Oh!" the sprite breathed again. "I've never seen such diamonds!"

Rosie smiled. The sprite simply could not

take her eyes from the glittering necklace.

"I must try it on!" The sprite declared, turning to a nearby servant. "Bring a mirror immediately!" she demanded. Then she waved her hand at the others who had brought gifts. "Take your presents away! I have made my decision. I will have these diamonds!"

Rosie heaved a silent sigh of relief and glanced at Hana, who was watching the sprite nervously.

"Fasten the necklace around my neck," the sprite ordered Rosie. "And be quick!"

A servant hurried over to the sprite and held a mirror in front of her while Rosie carefully lifted the necklace from its box.

It was so cold she could feel her fingers burning, but she willed herself not to show any sign that the jewels were made of ice. Swiftly, she walked over to the sprite and placed the diamonds around her neck.

"Oh!" the sprite gasped, as Rosie fastened the clasp. "The necklace is cold!" Then a smile spread across her face as she admired her reflection. "But it's so sparkly!"

Rosie looked at the sprite's reflection in the mirror, and saw that a tiny drop of water was forming on the end of one small diamond. As she watched, the droplet fell straight onto the sprite's smooth skin.

The sprite frowned and peered at her reflection. "What's that?" she asked. Then her eyes widened in horror as more of the ice

began to melt and tiny drops of water ran down her neck. "No!" she shrieked in fury. "NO!"

Her eyes blazing with anger, the sprite put her hands up to tear the necklace off. But her fingers immediately became wet too, and she wailed with rage. Rosie watched in amazement. She could see that the sprite was starting to shimmer slightly all over, like the ripples on a pool of water.

"Look!" shouted the man who had brought the rubies. He was pointing at the spot where Hana stood next to Rosie. "There's another princess appearing right there!"

Rosie turned to look at Hana. Other people were staring at the real princess too, just as if they could see her. Rosie realized that as the sprite was turning back to her original form, so Hana was slowly reappearing!

"This is the *real* princess!" Rosie shouted, pointing at Hana. "The river sprite took her place and made Hana invisible!"

The sprite glared at her. "Out of my way!" she cried, pushing Rosie aside and running from the room.

Everyone poured out of the ballroom after her, including Rosie and Hana. The sprite was heading through the gardens towards the river, and as she ran, she was becoming more and more translucent and shimmery.

Once the sprite reached the riverbank, she leapt lightly into the water without a moment's hesitation. As she did, she melted into a shower of raindrops, which pattered down into the water, sending ripples here and there. In a moment there was nothing left of the sprite except a handful of peach blossom floating on the surface of the water.

Rosie turned to look at Hana. Everyone was staring at the princess now, and Rosie realized that her friend was fully visible again.

"Hana, my child!" The emperor stepped forwards, his face alight with happiness. "You are restored to us!"

He and his wife hugged their daughter, while Rosie looked on, beaming.

"Father, this is my friend Rosie," Hana said, beckoning Rosie to join them. "It is because of her that I am free from the sprite's spell. But the sprite chose *her* gift, so you must

grant Rosie her heart's desire."

The emperor smiled kindly at Rosie. "I thank you for the help you have given my daughter," he said. "The sprite did indeed choose your gift, and now *you* must choose your reward. What is your heart's desire?"

Rosie didn't hesitate. "Please, Your Highness, I would like you to build a great temple to honour Gawa, the river god!" she replied.

"It shall be done!" the emperor said firmly. And at his words, Rosie saw the river water bubble and swirl with excitement.

"Now let us celebrate my daughter's birthday!" the emperor announced. "Musicians, strike up a tune!"

The musicians, who had followed the sprite along with everyone else, began to play. And there on the grassy riverbank, everyone started to dance.

"Come and dance with me, Rosie," Hana said with a smile.

"I don't know how!" Rosie declared, as she watched the princess's graceful hand movements.

"I'll teach you," Hana replied. She borrowed two painted fans from the court dancers and gave one to Rosie. Then Hana showed her how to open and close the fan, twirling it in different positions as she danced. "Imagine that you're a flower, swaying in a gentle breeze," she said.

Rosie found it quite hard to move the fan
and her feet at the same time, but after a little while she got the hang of it. By the time
the dancing finished, she was feeling quite
pleased with herself. Then, as everyone began

to file back to the
palace for the
banquet, she drew
Hana aside.

"Hana, I must
go home now," she
whispered.

Hana gave her
a hug. "Thank
you for everything,
Rosie!" she said
gratefully. "Will
you come back
soon?"

"Of course I
will," Rosie replied.
"I can't wait!
Goodbye!"

As soon as
the words were

out of her mouth, Rosie felt the whirlwind full of peach blossom spring up around her once more. And as she was lifted up into the air, Rosie just had time to wave goodbye to her Japanese friend.

In the blink of an eye, Rosie found herself back in front of the mirror in her turret bedroom, with Great-aunt Rosamund's fan in her hand. "I'm home!" Rosie said to herself happily. She glanced down at the fan. There was Hana, seated beneath the fragrant peach tree, but now she looked much happier.

Well, now I know what I'm going to do at the school show, Rosie thought. *A Japanese dance!*

Opening the fan, she began to practise the steps that Hana had shown her.

"Hey, Rosie, that looks great! How did you learn to dance like that?" Luke demanded, dashing into the room.

Rosie laughed. "I had a very good teacher!" she replied. And that was true — she'd been taught by a *real* Japanese little princess!

THE END

Did you enjoy reading about Rosie's
adventure with the Peach Blossom Princess?
If you did, you'll love the next
Little Princesses
book!

Turn over to read the first chapter of
The Rain Princess.

Chapter One

Rosie Campbell sat at the kitchen table in her great-aunt's castle. "These cookies are delicious, Mum," she said, licking chocolate off her fingers.

"Can I have another, Mum?" asked Luke, Rosie's five-year-old brother, reaching towards the plate.

"You'll go pop!" Mrs Campbell exclaimed. "You've already had two!"

"Three," corrected Rosie, who'd been counting. "*And* half the cookie mixture before we put it in the oven. Greedy guts!" she teased her brother.

Luke stuck his tongue out at her and then looked at their mum with wide blue eyes. "Please, Mum," he begged.

"All right," Mrs Campbell laughed, handing him another cookie. "But this is the last one or you won't have room for lunch."

"You shouldn't make such delicious biscuits, if you don't want us to eat them," Rosie said, quickly helping herself to another before her mum took the plate away.

"It's this wonderful kitchen," her mum replied, looking round at the huge castle kitchen. "It seems to make everything taste good." She smiled happily at Rosie. "You know, I still can't quite believe we're living here."

Rosie's adventures had started the day she and her family had moved in. Rosie had found a note from her great-aunt telling her to look out for "Little Princesses" who were hidden around the castle. Each time she found a princess, the note had told Rosie to curtsey and say "hello". The princesses could be anywhere – in a tapestry on the wall, in the painted detail on a vase, or even woven into the picture on a rug – but every time Rosie found one, she followed her great-aunt's instructions and was whisked away into an amazing adventure.

I hope I find another little princess soon, Rosie thought.

Just then, Mrs Campbell glanced out of the window. "Here's Rob with the post," she said.

Rosie looked and saw Rob, the cheerful young postman, parking his van on the drive outside. "I'll get it," she offered. She ran out of the kitchen, through the Great Hall, and heaved open the castle's heavy wooden door.

Rob came crunching over the gravel towards her. "Morning, Rosie," he said, handing her a pile of mail. "There are a couple of post-cards in there for you and Luke." He nodded at two postcards on the top of the pile. One had a picture of a pride of lions lying in the shade of a thorny tree, and the other had a picture of zebras grazing near a waterhole.

Rosie turned them over curiously. "They're from Great-aunt Rosamund!" she exclaimed, recognizing the curly handwriting.

It said,

To Rosie, my Little Princess,

I hope you are having a lovely time in the castle and enjoying LOTS of adventures. I'm on safari in Kenya at the moment. It is a very beautiful place — there are miles of wide flat grasslands called "savannah" and lots of animals. I hope you will see it all yourself one day. Keep looking out for those Little Princesses.

Lots of Love,

Great-aunt Rosamund

Rosie sighed. She really wished she could tell Great-aunt Rosamund about the adventures she'd been having. Staying in the castle was wonderful, but it would have been even better if her exciting great-aunt had been there too.

Just then, Rosie's dad came outside. "Was that the post?" he asked.

Luke nodded. "We've got postcards from Great-aunt Rosamund," he said excitedly, as Rosie handed their dad the other envelopes.

"She says she's in Kenya," Luke went on. "Where's that?"

"In Africa," Mr Campbell replied. "Why don't you get an atlas from the library and I'll show you?"

"I'll get it," Rosie offered, racing back into the castle. The library was one of her favourite rooms. It had shelves of books reaching all the way to the ceiling. To get to the highest books, you had to climb up a ladder that was on rails so it could slide along the shelves.

Rosie slipped into the library and soon spotted a large old atlas on a shelf just below the top one. She pushed the ladder towards it and climbed up to collect the atlas. As she did so, something caught her eye. At the back of the shelf, in the space where the book had been, there was a small dusty statue about the size of a milk bottle.

Rosie picked it up curiously. It was a figure of a girl carved out of dark wood. Her face was beautiful, but her eyes looked sad and she had a tear running down one cheek. The wood had been cleverly carved to show every detail of the girl's flowing robes and delicate headdress. Rosie felt a rush of excitement. Could this be another little princess?

Climbing quickly down the ladder, she placed the atlas and the statue carefully on the library desk. Then she dropped into a curtsey. "Hello," she whispered to the wooden statue.

The instant the word left her mouth, Rosie felt a warm breeze pick up and swirl around her. It smelt of hot earth and sun-baked grass. Rosie's heart beat faster; she was going on another adventure! As she shut her eyes, the breeze became a whirlwind which swept her up into the air.

A few moments later, Rosie felt herself touch down gently on the ground. A blanket of heat wrapped itself around her. She opened her eyes and gasped.

Flat, scrubby grassland stretched away in all directions. Only a few thorny trees stretched up from the ground, their branches silhouetted against the blue sky. Running across the grassland was a wide, shallow river with sun-baked, muddy banks and, in the distance, dark mountains marked the horizon.

A herd of zebra was grazing by the river. And Rosie realized with a gasp that the scene looked just like the picture of the savannah on Great-aunt Rosamund's postcard!

"Africa!" Rosie whispered to herself in astonishment. "I must be in Africa!"

Read the rest of *The Rain Princess* to follow Rosie's adventures!